A SONG IN THE NIGHT

DANIEL MILLS

A SONG IN THE NIGHT

MMXXIV

"On Christmas [...] Father and Mother were in Paris. Of their reunion Mother never spoke. Some things are too sacred to mention."

— Bertha Spafford Vester, *Our Jerusalem*, 1950

"How sad is my heart without my birds."

— Anna Spafford, *private writings*

PART ONE 11

PART TWO 35

PART THREE 49

PART FOUR 65

PART ONE

The woman is dead, drowned. *Inconnue*, a placard reads. *Unknown*. The flesh hangs pale and slack about the skull, dripping with cold, their faces in hers like light on the sea and sinking, disappearing in the fog of his breath on the window. Nine o'clock. His pocket-watch clicks against his palm and there's someone behind him, a man speaking French.

"It is Christmas," the attendant says. "You should not be here."

Spafford apologizes, explains. "The doors weren't locked," he says.

"I am expecting someone," the other man says, producing a cloth from his coat pocket and wiping Spafford's breath from the window. "Her father," he adds. "He came last night and recognized her. This morning he will take her home."

The drowned woman is one of three corpses on display in the morgue. The others are young men. The first is clean-featured and handsome but for the stubs of his teeth, a purple welt about his neck, while the other is badly scarred, a bullet-hole in his forehead. A rack above them holds the clothes they were found in. Shirts and jackets, a woman's gray dress.

"Marie Martin," the attendant says. "That is her name. Common enough, yes, as is her story. A girl comes to Paris with a young man. She becomes pregnant, but they do not marry. The young man leaves, goes where? She cannot say, is too ashamed to return home. She wanders the city, as if lost, and then there is the river."

"Where was she found?"

"Beneath the Pont Royal. The police pulled her from the water. She was not there long. An hour, perhaps."

"She jumped."

"Probably. It was early. No one saw it happen."

"How did she come to be here?"

"She had no handbag. The police found letters on her person, but the ink had run in the water, and the address could not be made out. They made inquiries, but no one knew her, who she was, so they brought her here. Hundreds have come to see her, but no one recognizes her, though many like you linger at the glass, watching, waiting—and for what, monsieur?"

The attendant's eyes on him, probing. The jets open into clouds of mist, a sound of breaking waves. He must get outside, get away. "I don't know," Spafford says, turning, allowing his feet to carry him out of the gallery and across the atrium.

But the other man calls after him. "Wait," the attendant says and disappears into his office, returning with a photograph that he places into Spafford's hands. Marie Martin. Eyes closed, her face as pallid and still as the others it holds inside.

The curve of Annie's mouth. Laugh-lines in her cheeks like Maggie or Bessie. Blue eyes like the baby Tanetta, their youngest. Born with the eyes of her mother, Anna, who didn't drown with them, who survived. *Saved alone*, she cabled. *What am I to do.*

"We did not know if anyone would come for her," the attendant says. "The cold water helps, but after three days, the dead must be buried. Her picture was to go in the cabinet."

He indicates a tall glass case in which unframed photographs show corpses in various states of putrescence. Most were found in the river, but others were victims of fire or industrial accidents, their bodies reduced to raw sinew, naked bone. Spafford glimpses himself among them, his reflection on the case, the sweat standing in drops on his forehead. He looks away, looks down at the photograph. Turns it over.

"You may keep it," the attendant says. "We have no need of it."

"I haven't, either."

The other man shrugs. *"Joyeux Noël,"* he says, and takes his leave, and Spafford slips the photograph into his coat. Water hisses in the pipes overhead. The jets open, drip, and he feels the force of gravity upon him, the planet's drag like an undertow.

*

Christmas morning, 1873. The girls are dead, and the world turns toward their absence, pulling him toward the Seine. He walks with his hands in his pockets, covering the dead woman's image, as his pocket-watch counts his steps across the Pont Neuf. Ten o'clock. Church bells burst like ordinance over the water and the sky sends back the echoes in circles that overlap and narrow about him to form a kind of cutting up which he proceeds, alone and aimless, following a train that has long since gone. It leads him to the Tuileries, the grand esplanade. He passes among the empty trees, their shadows in the dead leaves branching, crunching, and he is back in Chicago as it was before the fire in the early days of their courtship.

He was twenty-nine. Anna was sixteen. They met at a Sunday School in Chicago when Spafford taught a lesson on damnation and Anna lingered afterward to question him about hell. He quoted from scripture, what it says about Gehenna, but she shook her head. "You don't understand," she said, and he didn't, not then, or even weeks later, when they walked together in the evening, and she tried to explain what she had meant.

She was born in Norway, she said, but remembered nothing of the old country except the winters, the long dark. Her family booked passage to America when she was four and traveled to Chicago, taking the name of Lawson. Her mother died of cholera when she was young, and her father Lars contracted consumption in the years that followed. Bad air, the doctor said, and advised him to leave Chicago at once. Lars didn't delay. He purchased a homestead in Wanamingo, Minnesota, traveling overland in a wagon with Anna's brother Edward.

Anna, thirteen, did not accompany them. She remained in Chicago and boarded with a neighbor while attending Dearborn Academy. There she met Bertha Matteson, later Bertha Johnston, the doctor's wife. She had planned to stay through graduation, but Lars's condition worsened. *He's dying*, Edward wrote and pleaded with her to join them in Wanamingo.

She went to them, arriving in the fall. Edward and Lars lived in a one-room log cabin seven miles from the nearest homestead. The surrounding landscape was flat, oppressive, devoid of color or feature with few trees for windbreaks. Winter fell early there, as in Norway, and the snows became impassable. They drifted to the roof, sealing Anna inside with her father and brother. The men were taciturn by nature, little given to speaking and only then in Norwegian, which Anna had largely forgotten. She'd brought books with her from Chicago, gifts from the other girls at school, but found she couldn't read for the voice of the wind in the timbers, whispering her awake each morning and keeping her from sleep at night, as it howled down the endless hours of darkness in which her father snored in his sickbed and Anna huddled by the fire with her ears covered, watching the coals go out.

Lars died in the spring. The ice was out of the Mississippi, and Anna begged Edward's permission to return by boat to Chicago. He nodded, didn't argue. The next week, he drove her to an outlying farm that belonged to an elderly Norwegian couple. They lived there with an adult son, a Lutheran minister. This man had agreed to chaperone Anna to the ferry landing, but it would be another week before he was ready to depart: he had marriages to perform, children to baptize. He went off, then, entrusting Anna to the care of his aged parents. The old woman was blind and frail and suffered from dropsy while her husband was broad-shouldered and tall, a lecher with brass teeth who reeked of his own vitality.

He showed Anna to the attic, where she was to sleep. "Get undressed," he said in Norwegian, grinning through his false teeth and pawing at Anna until his wife's voice drifted up from downstairs. "I'll come back," he said, taking the candle, leaving her in the dark.

The attic slanted steeply with low eaves so she couldn't stand but crawled on her belly toward the sound of the wind. She reached the northern wall and scuttled along it until she reached a pile of foul straw where she burrowed in, tried to hide. The old couple argued downstairs, and the cold air slashed through gaps in the siding.

Somehow, she slept. Hours later, she awoke, a weight on her chest.

*

"I thought he'd come back," Anna said, "the old man. I struck out with my fists, hard, but the figure made no sound except for a kind of mewling. I tried to scream but couldn't, and there was a hand across my mouth. I bit at it until I tasted blood."

They had reached the end of their walk. A curdled moon hung over the house where Anna lived with her older half-sister: she watched them from an upper window.

"I must have fainted," Anna said. "Because I woke up, and it was morning, and a woman lay beside me. She was about thirty, maybe older. The dress she wore was all rags, and her long hair coiled about her middle like a serpent, coarse as the straw that covered us. She held a doll at her chest and slept with one arm thrown across me, the way a mother bird shelters its young."

"Who was she?" Spafford asked.

"The minister told me later that she was the old man's stepdaughter, his wife's child from a previous marriage. Born mad, her stepbrother said. Happy to spend her days in the nearby woods and her evenings in the attic. She played with her doll, talked to herself in Norwegian."

The light shifted. Anna's shadow appeared on the wooden slats between them, and Spafford looked back to the house, where her half-sister had lit a lamp, drawn back the curtain.

"I followed her once," Anna said. "Into the woods. She caught a rabbit in a trap she'd made and butchered it with her fingernails. She took a little meat for herself but fed the rest to her doll, which was propped against a fallen log beside her. The blood was everywhere, smeared on her face and hands and pooling in the dirt. It frightened me. I ran."

"She sounds a terrifying creature," Spafford says.

Anna didn't reply, didn't seem to hear.

He reached out with his hand, touched her shadow on the ground.

She shivered.

"Actually," she said, "she was quite sweet. A week later, the minister came back for me in the cart, and we drove off. The road skirted the woods, and that's where she was waiting for me. Her hands were red and bloody, but she beckoned for me to join her, to stay. I didn't speak, couldn't even look at her. The wagon rounded a bend in the road, and I began to cry."

His hand, outstretched, closes on nothing. Her hair's shadow streams between his fingers.

"Relief," Spafford said.

"No," she said. "Shame. Because I hadn't talked to her, hadn't thanked her for saving me. Don't you see? She was in the attic that first night. She had seen her stepfather grab at me. *I'll come back*, he'd said, and she had tried to protect me, joining me in the bed and sheltering me with her body even though I hit her with my fists. She wrapped me in those bloodied arms like bird's wings and I believed I was in hell."

"You were young," Spafford said. "You were scared."

"I didn't recognize her, what she was."

"No one can truly know another, what's inside their heart."

"No? Not ever?"

She turned to him. The streetlamp put sparks in her blue eyes, and he retreated from them, withdrawing beyond the rings of their illumination.

"In heaven, perhaps," he said. "When we are face to face."

"We're face to face now," Anna said, stepping toward him. "And you too would mistake heaven for hell. And run from it—from me—because you are afraid."

Another step, and she was with him in the dark. The sparks dropped out of her eyes and there was three feet between them, less. She slipped off her glove. She touched his face. He felt her warmth like a brand upon his cheek.

"I won't run," he said. "But I am afraid."

"I know."

"Aren't you?"

"A little," she said. "But not of you."

*

They were engaged in '58, married in '61. Anna's half-sister agreed to the match but only if the wedding were delayed so Anna could finish her schooling. Spafford assented and paid to send her to a ladies' seminary in Lake Forest, where he wrote her rambling letters and occasionally sent books of poetry and theology, gifts of jewelry and chocolate.

Three years. The engagement was long and never less than chaste, but Spafford often thought of the dark outside her half-sister's house and of Anna's hand on his cheek, the heat of it. The softness of her skin. *We're face to face now,* she'd said, and maybe she had believed it, but even now, after twelve years of marriage, they are as ignorant of each other as they were then, nearly strangers, no different from the courting couples that flood the Tuileries on Christmas morning.

The men sport frock coats and top hats, watchchains and whiskers. The women sparkle in their jewels and finery. Late morning, and the sunlight plays on their features as they approach and pass and do not see him. Spafford reaches the end of the esplanade, where there are drifts of brown leaves and stumps where trees once stood, felled by artillery during the Prussian siege or the violence that ended the Commune. The fencing is damaged, iron palings bent outward by a bursting shell but with room enough between for cats to come and go.

He's tired, hasn't slept properly in weeks. He sits on a tree-stump with his back to the fence and his head in his hands. Fruitmongers call to each other across Rue de Rivoli behind him and he can hear the screams of children, the clicking of his pocket-watch, the clangor of bells striking midday. He lifts his head, and the Palais des Tuileries swims into view, what's left of it, sunlit and shimmering, a steamer at rest on the ocean's bottom.

*

Bertha Johnston read about the disaster in the French papers. *Ville du Havre.* She recognized the name and telegrammed to the Cunard Line, who forwarded her message to Bertry, in the Nord, where Anna was staying with the family of Théophile Lorriaux.

The two women were old friends, schoolmates from Dearborn. Anna left Bertry the next day. The Johnstons met her at the Gare du Nord and wired ahead to Liverpool, where Spafford's ship was due, instructing him to join his wife in Paris.

Théo sent a separate wire. *Come to Bertry after Christmas,* he suggested, and Spafford wrote back to suggest the 28th, a Sunday. Théo replied to confirm the date. His letter reached Spafford in Paris, the Johnstons' apartments on Boulevard Malesherbes.

No. 10, a fashionable address. The family occupies an expansive suite of rooms on the second floor where Anna passes the long days of her infirmity, talking to birds no one sees, listening for songs nobody hears.

Spafford shrinks from her, cannot face her. Christmas Eve he spent with Bill Johnston in the surgery while the doctor's son Robert sprawled on the floor between them with the family's photo album. The boy leafed through postcards from New York and London, portraits from a studio on the Boulevard des Capucines: *Mayer & Pierson, Photographes de S.M. l'Empeurer.*

The men drank burgundy, then port, and Bill told him stories of the siege and of his time with the American Ambulance: lives he saved, those he couldn't. He talked about the Communards too and the Bloody Week in May of '71 when soldiers from Versailles forced the barricades and the rebels burned the city as they fled. Bill was at the American Legation when it happened, sleeping in the consul's office, when he woke to find the curtains full of light.

"The balcony looked out on the Tuileries," he said. "The palace was in flames, gashed down one side and spilling out smoke. No moon or stars but the fire made light enough to see the great dome falling, crashing in on itself in the moment before the roar of the explosion. The sound reached me where I stood, striking to my middle, and a mass of sparks heaved out of the rubble, whirling up in coils of smoke. In all my life, I own, I have never seen anything so terrible, so beautiful."

Three years later, and the palace is in ruins, an open wound, but Spafford is thinking of another fire, a different city, Chicago. Because the planet turned and turned them with it. Their Eden kindled, catching light, and Spafford was away on business. October 9, 1871. He wasn't there, can only imagine the dark of that morning when Anna stepped onto the porch of their house in Lake View. To the south the city had vanished behind a roiling cloud that poured itself out in currents, scattering coals like foam and setting roofs alight. The girls told him what happened next. How Anna ran inside screaming, saying they had to make ready. How they spent the night in a field outside the city, waking with the rain on their faces.

They were lucky. He thought so, anyway. For a time.

The house was spared, but Anna wasn't. She appeared much older, somehow, though only days had passed, and in the months that followed, she withdrew into herself, retreating to a place he could not follow. She wouldn't leave the parlor, wouldn't come to bed, banked the stove high and watched it burn to ashes. One night, late, he came down after the girls were asleep. He went to her in the parlor, and she did not refuse him, but he hated himself afterward, the face he had glimpsed in those eyes like sea-ice, a drowning man.

His own situation was becoming desperate. After the fire, he had speculated in property outside the city, but his investments declined in value, and he couldn't sell them, not even at a loss. He borrowed from banks, raising loans to cover the interest he owed, but his debts mounted, accumulating, and he couldn't tell anyone, had no one to tell.

Two years after the fire and Anna had withered into absence. Sleeping little, eating less. Spafford sent for a doctor, who pressed on her back and belly and listened to her breathing. Her health was sound, he said, declaring himself certain of her recovery. He suggested they might undertake a long sea voyage. A tour of the continent, perhaps?

"You mustn't begrudge the expense," the doctor said, and Spafford didn't, mortgaging the house to purchase staterooms aboard the steamer *Ville du Havre* departing from New York. He made arrangements for the girls to board in Switzerland and in France while he and Anna continued on alone, together, as they were in their Eden in the days before the girls, the fire. They were to spend a year or more in Europe, traveling, before returning to the States, but it never happened. They were all at breakfast in New York, preparing for their departure, when the bank telegrammed him from Chicago, threatening foreclosure and disgrace if he did not return there immediately. He folded the telegram, slipped it into this jacket. The girls didn't notice or else paid him no mind, chattering of this or that, but he felt Anna's eyes on him like long nails driven through. He cleared his throat. She didn't speak but only smiled sadly, as if she sensed, even then, the lateness of the hour.

*

Three o'clock: weak sun, bare trees.

He draws the photograph from his pocket, flattens it against his thigh. Annie and Maggie. Bessie and Tanetta. Again as in the morgue the girls surface in the lines and hollows of a dead woman's face, alive despite the planet's turning, the clicking of his watch. They aren't here, he knows that, but he isn't either, never was.

Chicago burned and he was away on business. Anna fell into madness and he hid in his office, drinking down the weight he carried.

He accompanied the girls as far as the harbor in New York, but he didn't join them as he had promised, and his fist is closing over the photograph as he stands up, running, outpacing the fall of twilight.

Boulevard des Capucines. His shoes ring on the paving, echo into the shade trees and streetlamps, but there are no lights in the windows of Mayer and Pierson, *Photographes de S.M. l'Empeurer.* He tries the door, but it isn't locked. The boulevard opens into brittle silence, a high-ceilinged salon with couches and divans and mirrors on the walls. A chandelier hangs above his head, unlit, a black star spinning out shadows.

He calls out. "Is anyone there?"

No answer, but there's a man stretched on a nearby couch, sleeping with ankles crossed on the arm of the settee. His suit is rumpled, badly creased, and his face is concealed by a fez.

"*Pardon*," Spafford says, but there's no response, and he lifts the fez to uncover the face of a young man of about twenty-five, who bolts up, startled, leaping to his feet and pawing with his sleeve at his mouth, the wine-stains on his lips.

"I'm sorry if I surprised you," Spafford says, holding out the fez.

The younger man takes it, places it on his head askew.

"No, no," he says. "It is nothing."

"This is the studio of Monsieur Pearson?"

"My father-in-law. You wish to schedule a sitting?"

"Please."

"I will fetch him."

The young man goes out. He reappears minutes later, looking suitably chastened, followed into the salon by an older man in his forties attired in scarlet fez and velvet waistcoat. The older man introduces himself as Monsieur Pierre-Louis Pierson.

"Forgive my son-in-law," he says. "He cannot help that he is young, but he has been too long indulged. Just this morning my own daughter calls me a slavedriver because I drag him from his bed at half-past ten. It's Christmas, she said, and so it is, but I am stubborn. The work is never finished, I said, and lucky for us that it should be so. Lucky for you too, Monsieur."

"I hope this isn't inconvenient."

"May I ask what brought you to my studio? You have seen my pictures of His Majesty? The Countess?"

"I'm staying with William Johnston. He's a client of yours, I believe."

"A remarkable gentleman, yes. And Madame Johnston is a most charming woman."

"She was at school with my wife."

"Will your wife join you? I understand you wish to make an appointment."

Spafford shakes his head. "I'm alone."

"Tomorrow morning, perhaps? Nine o'clock?"

"Is today impossible?"

Pierre-Louis considers. He suckles his moustaches, consults his pocket-watch. "It will be difficult," he says. "The light is failing."

"It's too late, you mean."

"No, monsieur. I mean we must be quick."

He takes off, loping, pausing only to beckon to Spafford to follow through a series of anterooms to a studio cluttered with elaborate costumes and plaster props, a row of windows facing an open courtyard, a purple sky.

"Stand there," the photographer says.

He points to a square rug beside the windows, and Spafford does as he is told, placing his cap on the couch behind him and resting his elbow on the stand.

Pierre-Louis retrieves a mirror and positions it opposite the windows, tilting the glass upon its axis until it catches the dusk and glows with it. "Enough," he says, murmuring to himself. "Enough." Then turns his attention to Spafford's clothing, tucking in and smoothing down, stepping back to survey his handiwork. He nods, satisfied, and retreats beneath the hood to prepare the plate, adjust the lens.

His voice comes muffled through the fabric. "You are ready?"

"Yes."

The flash-box explodes in light. Spafford, blinded, twitches reflexively, and the photographer whistles through his teeth.

"Your hat," Pierre-Louis says. "Please take hold of it."

"My hat?"

"It will help you to keep still."

Spafford takes up his hat, digs in his nails.

"Like that, yes."

Pierre-Louis turns back to the camera, readies a second plate. Spafford's reflection hangs in the long mirror, face pale and shining. The studio's darker now and he can just make out a portrait on the wall behind him. It is that of a young woman with her face half-hidden by a folding picture frame, one eye looking out.

"You see the Countess?" Pierre-Louis asks. "In the mirror?"

The Countess of Castiglione. A famous beauty, Spafford recalls, at one time the mistress of Napoleon III.

"Yes."

"Look at her, please. And do not move."

Spafford breathes, holds the air in his lungs. The room fades into the Countess's photograph, black but for the eye that finds him, piercing him as the flash-powder ignites and the shutter clicks open and shut. He blinks. His sight returns but the mirror is dark, devoid of form or shape where it cannot hold the light, where there's no more light to hold.

"Much better," Pierre-Louis says. "It will be a fine portrait."

"I worried I had come too late."

"Not at all. The Countess herself often insists on evening light."

"She is still in Paris?"

"An apartment in Place Vendôme, yes, but she rarely goes out. The city she knew is in ashes, but there are times when I see it in the Countess herself, its light, such shining as she carries inside her."

They return to the grand salon where Pierre-Louis's son-in-law has lit the lamps to reveal the painted ceiling, a pastoral scene: trees in autumn colors and a dying hart sprawling, head upraised, as if to plead with the circling hounds. The huntsman follows close behind, mounted on a white horse and carrying a trumpet, but the paint is flaking, and his face is missing, a swath of damp.

The son-in-law produces a ledger. He takes down Spafford's name, the Johnstons' address. He tells Spafford he can expect to receive the *carte-de-visite* no later than the day after tomorrow. Money is exchanged. The younger man writes out a receipt and Pierre-Louis asks to be remembered to Dr. Johnston and his family.

"Good day to you, Monsieur Spafford," he says, bowing. "Or is it good evening?"

*

Nightfall, Place de la Madeleine. Streetlamps stain the white church yellow, the color of old bone. An ossuary, he thinks. Another morgue. Fenced against the living while the funeral march goes on with only a lone priest in attendance, an old street preacher. The man is tall and lean, almost skeletal, attired in black rags and battered top hat. His beard is gray and unkempt, flecked with spittle where it hangs to his waist. He spreads his arms, shrieks in a language Spafford doesn't understand. Spanish? He stinks of sewer gas, the abattoir. The crowd avoids him, parts round him like the waves about a rock, and Spafford would do the same, except for the girl. She's ten or eleven, Annie's age. She kneels on the pavement with hands folded in prayer and face lifted to the streetlamps that gutter and flare and crown the priest with a seraph's radiance. Two policemen detach themselves from the crowd, take the old man in hand. The preacher makes no protest, only smiles, and his eyes meet Spafford's through the crowd. His mouth drops open, showing black teeth, gums, but his words, if there are words, are lost to the scrape of footsteps, voices, sounding brass. Spafford looks for the girl, but he doesn't see her and doesn't move though the funeral march continues and the crowds flow past the Madeleine, following the planet's turning, going round and round.

*

Spafford rings the bell, waits. The concierge appears, mumbling to himself as he unlatches the doors and shows him in. Upstairs the gallery is black and oppressive but for lines of light beneath closed doors. Bertha Johnston sits alone in the dining room with a wineglass in hand and the evening's supper under a silver dome. The room smells faintly of mushrooms and two bottles stand empty on the sideboard behind her. Bertha rises, smooths down her skirts. "Can I offer you a drink? The claret is gone, I'm afraid, but there's whiskey in the tallboy."

Spafford accepts. He serves himself a cold supper of bread and thin soup while Bertha takes down a tumbler and pours a double portion. They clink their glasses together, drink.

He thanks her for the nightcap.

"A nightcap?" Bertha says. "Is it as late as that?"

He checks his pocket-watch. Half-past-eight.

"Maybe not," he says.

"You were up early. Bill heard you go out."

"I couldn't sleep," he says. He doesn't talk about the morgue, wouldn't know how to explain, but because Bertha is quiet, expectant, he tells her about the Madeleine and the street preacher raving in a language he didn't recognize.

"Occitan," she says.

"I'm sorry?"

"We saw him too. Earlier today. The cab stopped near the Church of Saint-Laurent and he came up to the window. He wanted money, I thought, but he only reached into the carriage and touched Anna's hand. Then he bowed to us and took himself away."

"Was he alone?" Spafford asks, thinking of the girl outside the Madeleine.

"I should think so. An anchorite, Monod called him. Defrocked, excommunicated. Inexplicably living in Paris."

Théo Monod. Years ago, the young pastor had ministered to the Indians in Kankakee, Illinois, where Spafford first made his acquaintance. Monod has since returned to Paris, and three days ago called at the Johnstons' apartments to offer his condolences. Anna laughed them off and invited him to sing American Sunday School hymns with her at the pianoforte. She even asked after Monod's children, taking down their names and ages and later buying them Christmas gifts at the Bon Marché, which she insisted on delivering in person.

"Did Monod say anything else?" Spafford asks.

"Nothing of importance. Naturally, he was surprised to see us. Discomfited, even, but he invited us inside and asked us to stay for supper. I told him we couldn't, that Bill was expecting us. A lie, as it happened, but it seemed the best thing. The kindest, anyway."

"The kindest," Spafford says. "Yes."

He reaches for the tumbler, takes a mouthful of whiskey. He chokes it down. Shudders at the heat that traverses his chest to his gut before boiling up again, filming on his gums and teeth as he clears his throat, asks, "Where is she now?"

Bertha shakes her head. "In bed, I think. We're taking the first train to Versailles."

Spafford stands, goes to the window.

Daniel Goodwin is due in Paris. An attorney like Spafford but possessed of a flourishing practice where Spafford has only debts. The two men have known each other for years. They are friends, Daniel might say, but Spafford envies the younger man his money and success, his beautiful wife with her shrill laugh like a cart's wheel screeching.

Mrs. Goodwin children lost, Anna cabled from Cardiff. *Saved alone.*

Spafford wired back instructions, and the two men traveled together to New York, sharing a stateroom aboard the *Abyssinia*. They parted ways in London with Spafford continuing to Paris while Daniel remained in England to attend the Board of Trade inquiry.

Three days ago, Daniel wrote to Spafford to inform him he was coming to Paris after all and planned to arrive on the 26th. A short visit only, Daniel explained, but he hoped he might speak to Anna. He needed to know how it happened, what it was like, but Spafford replied to say she was away, out of town, and might they meet with Nathaniel Weiss instead?

Afterward, Spafford approached Bertha to see if she would take Anna away from Paris, if only for a night or two. Bertha agreed. The Johnstons have friends in Versailles, she explained, and Anna had wanted to see the palaces since their time at Dearborn when the girls had daydreamed of masked revelers and royal balls, the Petit

Trianon which the dead queen loved.

"I'll write today," Bertha said. "I'll tell Mary to expect us after Christmas."

"Thank you," Spafford said—says.

Bertha smiles, sadly, and drains her glass. A carriage passes on the boulevard, dragging its shadow behind it. The sounds fade, wheels and hoofbeats and the snap of the coachman's whip, and Spafford hears laughter from upstairs, voices from another room. Bill, Robert.

"It won't last," Bertha says. "Her—condition."

"Condition," he says. "We may call it that, I suppose."

"She is still herself. She isn't mad."

Spafford says nothing. His glass is nearly empty. A candle-flame swims in the liquid, shifts with the roll of the tumbler between his fingers as he lifts the glass to his lips and swallows it down, all of it, whiskey and fire together, and there's tears in his eyes as he turns from the window, saying, "No? Then how do you explain it?"

His tone is acid. His voice cracks, but Bertha is kind.

"See it like a shadow," she says, gently. "A mountain so high it blocks the sun. Such peaks cannot be scaled: they can only be outlasted. And that's all she is doing, Horatio, albeit in her way, as you are doing it in yours."

"And failing."

"You're here, aren't you? Maybe that's enough."

*

Bertha wishes him goodnight, retires to her room. Spafford pours another drink and downs it before going out. No one in the gallery. Anna, it seems, is in bed, and the door to the guest room is closed. He passes Robert's bedroom and hears Bill inside, reading aloud by the light of a fairy lamp. "'Near to the winter fire,'" Bill reads, "'sat a beautiful young girl, so like the last that Scrooge believed it was the same...'"

Christmas Past. Last year in Lake View he put the girls to bed and waited until they were asleep before going downstairs and pulling on his boots. Minus ten degrees and the snow lay thick on the ground, squeaking beneath his feet as he trudged toward the road with its row of ornamental elms. One of the trees was diseased, dying. The girls played post office there, hiding letters in the hollow for one another to find. Annie, his eldest, checked the tree every morning for letters, even in winter, crossing the yard in her galoshes and always by the same path so her footprints deepened in time, hardening, brimming with his shadow as he followed in her steps with the dolls beneath his arm, wrapped in butcher's paper, a mother and father and four young girls, their hair cut short like theirs. He placed the package into the hollow then returned the way he came, turning in the doorway to a world awash in silver, moon on snow, and no new footsteps, no sign to show he had been there.

Bill's voice: "'He turned upon the Ghost, and seeing that it looked upon him with a face, in which in some strange way there were fragments of all the faces it had shown him…'"

He thinks of the drowned woman, Marie Martin, and of her image in his pocket. His fingers close round it, as if to cover her face, the faces it holds, but the parlor door opens behind him, and he's caught, can't hide, the girls forming themselves again out of the curves of Anna's smile as she crosses the threshold and takes his hand in hers.

*

Pine pitch and orange rind, scents of a home that no longer exists. The Johnstons' tree nearly fills the parlor, exceeding seven feet in height and crowned with a felt star, black, studded with pearl buttons. Ivy cuttings are scattered about the stand while the branches are laden with tinsel and citrus, gingerbread men hooked like fish by their mouths and hanging, helpless as he is with Anna's hands around his, drawing him inside.

She closes the door. The room dims, blurring into shadows, but he doesn't speak. Anna crosses to the hearth and kneels before it to rake out the ashes, to set the new coals blazing. The flames kindle and leap, driving back the dark, and she's closer now, advancing on him in the dress she has worn since Cardiff when the steamer company purchased mourning garb for the survivors and Anna would only wear white. The dress is muslin, plain, but she's radiant with the light behind her and hair pinned back in ribbons, pale blue, the color of her wedding gown. She's thin, too thin. The cords of her wrist protrude from her sleeves, tendons showing in the hand she places in his arm's crook. Her long fingers curl to his inner elbow, resting lightly, a weight he cannot shake. It drags him under, pulls him toward the Johnstons' tree with its ornaments blazing, mirrors for the fire's light. "Look," she says and takes down a cheap necklace, steel chain and gold paint and paste stones meant for sapphires. Children's jewelry.

"They left this for me," she says. "It's lovely, isn't it?" she asks, and puts it on, blocking the light with her body so the stones appear drained and dull. He steps back into the tree. The trunk lists to one side, upsetting the felt star, and a fake bird's nest slides to the end of the branches above him, where it stops, snarled in a web of needles, a stuffed finch staring out.

"Above you," Anna says. "There's something for you as well."

He looks up past the finch, spies a watch-chain in the branches. A paper tag dangles from it, marked with Anna's handwriting. *Merry Christmas*, it reads. He takes it down. The chain is brass and cheaply made, the kind of thing the girls might have bought with their pocket-money. Its loops roll on his fingertips, twitching as they catch the light then flipping the tag to its reverse, the words Anna wrote there. *From the children.*

"Don't you see?" Anna said. "She remembered."

*

Last September. A chill in the air and Anna's health in decline. The nursemaid Nicolet had taken the older girls outside and he was alone in his study with the infant Tanetta while Anna slept in the parlor, or didn't sleep, as was often the case, but watched the daylight cross the ceiling, expanding, contracting, edging away. Spafford sat at his desk with his legs pressed together and Tanetta between them. He bounced her between his knees, leaning forward to touch his face to hers. She giggled and flailed at his waistcoat, pocket-watch.

Her hand caught in the chain. The links coiled fast about her fingers, but she only looked at Spafford placidly and with such trust as he couldn't imagine, didn't deserve. He broke the chain. The next day he sold the pieces to a pawnbroker and said nothing of it to Anna, to anyone.

Weeks later, at breakfast, Bessie asked him about the watchchain. She was four and much taken with it, the way its links passed the light between them. Spafford lied, said he had misplaced it. Bessie told him not to worry. "I'll find it for you," she said.

He laughed. Bessie did too, though she couldn't understand the reason. They laughed together and didn't stop until Anna came in, and the silence with her. But she must have overheard them, Spafford realizes, because Anna's behind him now, close, easing the chain from his fingers and fastening the end to his waistcoat.

He smells her hair, feels her breath on the back of his neck. He tastes it too, clouds of it in the air between them as he turns and rips the chain from his waistcoat, throwing it down. The pieces scatter on the hearthrug, and he's shouting at her, cursing her, telling her she has to stop, that she's hurting him, that he needs her.

"They needed you too," she says, "my birds. Where were you?"

∗

Past midnight and Spafford sprawls across the bed, half-dressed, while Anna plays the piano in the parlor. A familiar tune, but he cannot place it. The notes tinkle softly as Anna's voice drifts across them, doubling the chords, as if to harmonize with another singer he cannot hear. He covers his head with a pillow and wills himself to vanish, to sink beneath the churning of his blood to a place of perfect stillness. A depth he cannot reach like the silence she inhabits and with which she sings in harmony while his pocket-watch ticks against his chest. It measures the space that divides them, broad as the Atlantic and deeper than the twelve years of their marriage or the thirty years between them that they lived: their girls, her birds.

He recalls *A Christmas Carol*, Belle in her house with her family gathered round while Scrooge, dreaming, looks on from outside. The past made present, as it is tonight, with Anna singing to the dead and Spafford drifting off, watching Annie return to the house last Christmas with the package under her arm. She runs upstairs to wake her sisters, and later, he finds the girls in the nursery with the dollhouse open and the new dolls arranged in the parlor, heads bent toward one another, as in some game, while a fifth doll, their mother, reclines in a rocking chair beside a paper fire. "Where am I?" he asks, and Maggie points to an upper room, where a bespectacled figure sits at a writing desk with the door closed, as if to shut out the music of their laughter from downstairs or of all the churches in Paris striking one o'clock.

He doesn't hear them, doesn't wake.

He dreams of shore-bells clanging, ships in fog.

PART TWO

Hôtel Vouillemont. The garçon shows him to a courtyard where a string quartet plays Vivaldi, *Prima Vera*. Daniel Goodwin sits beneath the overhang. He has his back to the door and a porcelain dish at his elbow with a lit cigar inside, smoldering. The men shake, sit, smoke.

Daniel inquires after Anna. "I wish she could have joined us."

Spafford explains she is in Versailles, spending two nights with friends of Bertha. "Her condition is much improved," he says.

The quartet climaxes, rests, and the courtyard falls quiet. Foreign voices, hushed laughter. Nathan Weiss is late. Spafford asks Daniel about the upcoming Board of Trade inquiry, if he is still planning to attend?

Daniel nods. "Useless, of course, but I have to go. The French blame the English, the English blame the French, and nothing is done, no one's responsible. It's the way of these things, I know, but I cannot accept it. 226 dead. Someone must be to blame."

"Yes."

"But who?"

Nathan arrives. The Frenchman's beard is well-oiled, his attire impeccable, but his temple is yellow with faded bruising, and he wears about him a look of exhaustion or resignation as he crosses the courtyard and takes Spafford's hand, squeezing.

"My friend," he says.

Five weeks have passed since they last saw one another and that was in America where Nathan had traveled in the company of Théo Lorriaux and another French pastor named Emil Cook. The Three Musketeers, they called themselves, all for one and one for all, but only Nathan is left in Paris.

Daniel thanks him for coming, invites him to sit. The garçon appears, but Nathan waves him off and slips a hand into his coat to withdraw his tobacco pouch and pipe. The shag he smokes is sour and strong. "The army," Nathan explains. "Here, in France, the young men all must serve. This *tabac* it was all we had, but you become used to a thing, do you not?"

"Some things," Spafford says.

"Yes," Nathan says. "That is so."

The quartet returns to the courtyard's center. The men resume their chairs, take up their instruments. They count in silence, bows and fingers poised: one, two, three.

*

I am a teacher of the Sunday School, Nathan says. It is for me a calling, and I serve the *Societé des Écoles du Dimanche* as its agent in Paris. But the Sunday School is new to us in France and we must look to America and men like yourselves. We have learned so much from you, gentlemen, from your churches and schools. Your children, too.

Sunday morning was our second day aboard the *Ville du Havre* and Emil had the idea to host a little Sunday School aboard ship. The weather was good, and the children were excited. Madame Spafford was in attendance, I recall. Your children as well, Monsieur Goodwin, Lulu and little Goertner. Emil saw to everything.

He arranged the saloon while we were at luncheon so that we came down to find two long tables pushed together beneath a tablecloth, red with white flowers like lilies. Emil seated himself at the head of the table with the children to either side. Goertner and Lulu sat opposite Annie and Maggie with their mothers behind them and the nursemaid Nicolet.

Emil prayed, the children sang. The lesson, I remember, was from Matthew 18, the unmerciful servant, when Christ tells Peter he must forgive seventy-times-seven. Emil asked the children how many times they must give pardon, and it is your daughter, Monsieur Spafford, little Annie, who answers. *Four hundred and ninety*, she says. Emil smiles—kindly, you understand—and he gives perhaps a little laugh, but Annie is red like the cloth and redder still when her younger sister Maggie says, *Always. Because Christ pardons always.*

Afterward we went above deck. The sea was calm, the stern all in froth as the screw turned and turned in it. The spray slapped at us, our faces. Théo returned below decks, but I remained, wishing to watch the ladies at their promenade and the children running and sliding with arms held out. The sun was setting, a column of fire at our backs, and the first stars were in the east. You can imagine, gentlemen, how it was? The perfection of the evening?

Théo and I retired to our berths. In the night we were awakened by the sound of wind at the bulkhead, the ship tossing wildly. Théo lifted the deadlight to look out but all was darkness and roaring, nothing to be seen but the black peaks of waves rolling toward us.

How slowly the night passed. In the morning the steward came in with coffee and we took this black for our stomachs. Théo and I met Emil in the saloon, but many others were absent. *Le mal de mer*, we thought, sea sickness, but we were wrong.

The American ladies, Madames Goodwin and Spafford and Bulkley, they had taken breakfast on the deck with their families and there had for themselves a jolly *pique-nique* in the wind. We joined them outside, but the weather was worse, colder now, and the gulls were screaming. A dreadful sound, but we made a merry company, laughing and shouting to be heard over the wind in the masts and the waves against the ship's bow.

Until a big wave took us, and the ship dropped with it, and all the deck chairs were overturned. We were piled together, all of us in a heap, but no one was hurt, and the girls were laughing when they stood, their faces wet with the spray and shining with it.

I recalled our little Sunday School, the song they sang. *I want to be an angel and with the angels stand / a crown upon my forehead, a harp within my hand.* Little Lulu suggested it, but they knew the song, all of them, and sang it with great feeling. So bright the flame they held inside. It was a blessing to share that morning with them, to see the light leap from their faces and from the eyes of the ladies too, their mothers, especially Madame Goodwin.

Your wife, Monsieur Goodwin, she is like a girl herself with arms raised and shouting for joy as another wave strikes us and we are soaked. I asked her if she was quite comfortable, if she wished to retire below-deck? She only laughed. That laugh she had like a sea-bird's crying out.

But for Madame Spafford it is different. Your girls, monsieur, they gather round their mother's chair dancing. Annie rocks the babe upon her knee and the babe is yelling. *Up and down,* she screams, laughing, but Madame Spafford doesn't smile.

Later, I ask Théo about her, and he tells me what I suspected, that her health is poor, her nerves, and that it was for this reason she has taken this journey. Your doctor advised it, I understand, but the ocean, it is changeable, as are the moods of a drinker, gentle in the morning and cruel at night, indifferent to anything but itself. It does not listen. Rarely speaks but to scream with its voice of waves and howling wind. For a day and a night the sea batters the ship's hull until the screw is damaged and we are all quite sick.

At last, the storm passes but the fog is like none I have experienced. The sea cannot be seen. The waves cannot be heard. Two days of this, gentlemen, and the cold it gets inside you. You stink of salt. Your clothes, hair, hands. Day and night, asleep or waking, it is always the same. You lie in your berth and shiver. The screw thumps and you sleep a little. You dream of fog and the foghorn's bellowing and again you are awake.

Friday the twenty-first. Théo woke me up, called for me to join him at the porthole. The sky beyond the ship was wide and blue and red gold at the horizon where the sun sat. The foghorn was quiet, the waves like plains of copper spreading.

We dressed for breakfast, which we took in the saloon. Théo called for champagne and the steward brought a bottle. We poured glasses for ourselves and toasted the health of the American ladies who sat near to us. Madame Goodwin laughed and returned the toast though her cup held only water. Madame Bulkley did the same and Madame Spafford too so that the saloon soon was in an uproar, all of us laughing and toasting one another.

You see how it was. The fog made madmen of us all.

In the evening I took my walk on the deck. A cold night, clear, and I lingered near the stern with the waves below me and the heavens spread with stars from end to end.

Madame Spafford joined me at the rail. She was alone, I noticed, and I wished her good evening. I made some remarks about the weather, but she was looking at the stars. She told me she had been ill. The world, she said, held nothing but pain. I tried to reassure her, saying we would soon be in France, but she only shivered and told me she was frightened.

God is good, I said. *The stars are beautiful, and why is this? Because He made them. He set the stars in the heavens and made them to burn and the sea also is His creation. You must trust in His goodness.*

She nodded and said that she would try. *If you could only know how good they are to me*, she said. *How kind they are, my birds. I do not deserve them. For years I could not see them, did not hear them for the roar of the hurt inside—and still they love me.*

Yes, Madame, I said.

I cannot understand it, she said.

No, Madame, I said, only that, but it seemed to comfort her. We watched the stars until the bells struck watch and we returned to our staterooms. Théo was awake, I recall, and I shared a drink with him before retiring to my berth at around eleven.

*

I am asleep and then I am awake. I do not know why until the noise comes again, metal on metal but louder this time, like an exploding shell, and of such force that I am shaken from my berth and Théo too. We aren't hurt, but something is wrong. The screw thumps once and is silent. The stateroom is dark. I fumble for my matches but cannot find them and Théo is on his feet. He goes to the door and looks out. The Captain is coming down the passage. *A vessel has struck us,* he says, but we mustn't worry, *non,* it is nothing. *And the engine?* Théo asks, but the Captain doesn't answer. Others call to him in English but he ignores them and Théo's voice is shaking when he returns to the stateroom and says we must go above deck.

We dress in the dark. The passage is crowded with men and women in nightclothes with the look of sleep about them. They are confused, as are we, but in all things, courtesy prevails. Stewards run past and the passengers do not detain them. Of some they ask with great politeness whatever is the matter, what has happened, and the answer is always the same. *Nothing, Monsieur, it is nothing.*

We go up and the deck is a scene of chaos. Bitter cold, no clouds to catch the day's warmth. The lamps are out, but the stars are like signal fires burning overhead as the crewmen rush between the lifeboats, shouting, and we happen upon a passenger in nightdress, an American. He has hold of a long wooden beam and with it strikes at the life preservers, trying to free them. I ask him if a man has gone overboard? He is white-faced and wild. *A man overboard?* he says. *You do not realize we are sinking?*

I will fetch a knife, I say, and I am turning back toward the stair when Théo gives a shout. He points to starboard where a sailing vessel can be seen. It is square-rigged, a clipper. The ship that struck us, no doubt, but there are no lights aboard and only its outlines can be made out. The sea between us is a mess of stars: their brightness dazzles. A seaman hurries past, but I catch hold of his elbow and ask if our ship is much damaged? He tells me I must not worry. Always it is the same assurances, the same words, and all lies.

We hear a heavy splash to port. One of the boats has launched half-empty. The Captain is yelling now, cursing the mate, and the deck is more crowded. Passengers swarm about the little boats while some crewmen keep them back and others work to free the boats. Théo excuses himself to return below-decks and I look back to the American at the buoys. Somehow he has got hold of one and stands at the railing with the ring about his middle, waiting.

Théo reappears. Madame Spafford is at his side and she has the baby in her arms. Mademoiselle Nicolet comes too and the three older girls follow with their friend Willie Culver. We are all together, then, far back from the boats, and Madame Spafford loops her arm through mine. *Promise you'll stay with us*, she says, and I do, I promise that. Maggie and Annie are holding hands and little Bessie is afraid. She grabs me about the legs, and her eyes spark with the light of the stars in them.

The dear child. Her gown is so thin. I tell her I will get for her a coat and hasten below-decks to our stateroom. My overcoat I take for Bessie and gather up shawls and blankets for the others. Then I go upstairs to the vestibule where I encounter Emil, who is hurt. He wanders the ship as one does in a dream but dressed only in his nightclothes. He is wet, soaked, and he smells of the sea. His stateroom, he says, was broken in by the collision. The sea poured inside and rose so quickly he was nearly drowned. I ask him of Madame Goodwin, for her stateroom is near his, but he does not know, he has not seen her. By now others are gathering in the vestibule and again they do not shout or shove but huddle together in their blankets to wait for what must come. Madame Bulkley is there with her daughter, Lallie, who holds her mother's hands and speaks to her words of comfort as she leads her toward the deck and I follow with Emil.

Come, I say. *We must go.*

The Captain is in a state. His daughters cling to him crying. A priest wanders the deck offering absolution to any in need of it before removing his surplice and hastening to starboard where the boats they are being loaded. I follow him to find Théo there with the Madame Spafford. The crush is dreadful. *Women and children*, the crewmen call, but the men they are like beasts. Théo wrestles with them. He tries to force a way for Madame Spafford, but she is frightened, will not fight, and everyone is shouting now or screaming in their panic—all but your girls, Monsieur, who do not cry out though the ship lists and groans.

To port, Théo says. *Quickly!*

We run. I have hold of Annie and Maggie by their hands. I drag them clear of the boats as the mainmast falls and the mizzen with it. The boats explode into sawdust and planking. The air is a hell of splinters. But the wind blows clear the dust and there is no more screaming. Only the moans of the wounded, the dying. Théo calls out to me. We are both cut, and badly, but your girls, monsieur, they are not hurt. They pray with us. For us. They comfort us as the deck tilts to the ship's listing and their mother stares at nothing with the baby at her chest awake and watching. Little Tanetta. She sees everything, it seems, and is not afraid, though the ship founders and rolls and we are falling, Lord, falling—

*

Into the sea, stars. 47°21'N 35°31'W.

Two weeks ago, a clear night in mid-ocean. The *Abyssinia*'s steward knocked at the door of the stateroom Spafford shared with Daniel. The Captain wanted them, he said. They dressed in haste and followed the steward to the captain's quarters, where they found the man engaged upon his nightly reckoning. He invited them to sit as he blotted the log and blew the page dry.

"Brandy?" he asked, producing a bottle and glass. The lamp swung in its fixture, putting diamonds in the brandy then putting them out again as the Captain raised his head, cleared his throat, gently laid the blow. "I have checked my figures," he said, "and there is no mistake. We are passing over the place where the *Ville du Havre* went down. She lies under our feet."

The lamp swung forward, back. Darkness rushed at Spafford, and he fled, bursting out of the cabin into the iron cold of the night. He climbed the deck-rail and looked down to the water, steadying himself with his arms extended. The railing pulsed in his shoes, hummed in his joints and sinews. The moon threw his shadow to the horizon, dark as the deeps three miles down, where he imagined them standing on the shattered deck with hands joined and faces upturned to the *Abyssinia* passing over. Keel, rudder, and screw. Spinning against the waves like the wheel of a ship's hatch turning, opening into silence.

*

The breath in his lungs. The watch in his hand like a Catholic's Saint Christopher, clenched in his fist so the winding crown digs at his palm, drawing blood. Its gears turn as the spring unwinds, as yet unexhausted, though the quartet have packed their instruments and departed and the garçon walks between the tables with a snuffer, extinguishing the candles.

"The waters rushed toward us," Nathan says. "I took hold of little Bessie and of Maggie too and said they must not let go. But the cold struck us like a hammer and I could not hold on. The ship pulled us down. The bow broke into pieces around us and there was planking and tangled lines and men and women kicking. My head was struck, I think, for I cannot recall what happened next. Only that I was alone when I awoke."

Nathan exhales. His pipe has burned down in the dish. Shadows gather in the wound he carries above his brow, and his eyes are damp.

"The sea that night was a hell of flailing arms and broken bodies, madmen fighting each other over bits of plank without even the breath to speak as the cold settled into us. Many gave themselves up to it, but I thought of your girls, Monsieur Spafford, and of the light they had inside them. The waves washed over me, turning me onto my back so that I saw the stars above me shining with the same light, which was theirs. I reached out my hand, as though to touch them, but caught instead at a drifting buoy, something to hold, and was saved."

Something to hold, Spafford thinks, as the winding crown snaps in his hand, cutting deep. The broken watch squirms against his skin, greased with his blood and moving like a thing alive as the last candle goes out and the dark draws down around them, black as the afterimage on a burned eye.

The hour is late, and Nathan's story is finished. Daniel stands and thanks him for speaking with them. "It is a comfort to know how it happened. To know they were asleep. That they didn't suffer."

"The Lord is not always kind," Nathan says. "But he is never cruel. You must try to believe that. Goodnight, monsieur, and *bonne année.*"

1874. The New Year stretches before them, leaden and gray as the ocean's skin with no horizon visible, no wind to hasten the crossing.

*

Daniel turns up his collar, suggests a walk. Spafford agrees and the two men strike south from the hotel, passing through a group of drunks in silks and toppers led by a woman in red tulle. She leaps from foot-to-foot, spinning, a bottle of wine in each hand, dancing up the street, while the men pay her attendance and the police, watching, do not intervene.

Place de la Concorde. The wind is stronger here, the river out of sight. Spafford leads Daniel across the plaza to the Quai des Tuileries where there are no carriages to pass them, no boats on the river. The water murmurs to itself beneath the lashing wind and there's no sound but their footsteps on the paving, their breath like clouds unraveling.

Daniel pauses. "It's beautiful here."

"It is."

"How I wish they might have seen it. Goertner. Lulu."

Spafford cannot picture Daniel's children. Their faces pass like smoke through his fingers.

"Do you know," Daniel says, "I often think they *can* see it. That they aren't at the bottom of the Atlantic at all but somewhere much nearer. I even find myself talking to them, telling them such stories as I would never have told them in life."

Spafford asks: "Are they with us now?"

"Just behind me," Daniel says.

"And you do not turn around?"

He shakes his head. "I know what I would see."

"And what is that?"

"The same as you, Horatio. No one. Nothing."

*

Not even stars. For ten years or more he couldn't see them, didn't believe in them. Spafford was nearsighted as a child though no one knew of it until one night in summer when he borrowed his cousin's spectacles and looked up through them at a sky he no longer recognized.

The night appeared as a sea of star-fire with constellations like drowned shapes glimpsed through the Milky Way's uncoiling, plunging toward him, a breaking wave. He cried out, frightened. He reached for his cousin's hand, as if to seek for purchase, and Daniel's hand, too, is clamped over Spafford's arm, his voice low and urgent.

"My God," he says. "What was that?"

The scream comes again, a child's wailing cry that catches in the treetops overhead. The Jardin des Tuileries runs alongside them, screened from view by a high wall and a row of bare trees with wind in their branches like tossed bones rattling. The trees whisper and screech and Spafford is scrabbling at the wall, splintering his fingernails, reopening the gash in his palm.

His grip fails, but Daniel is below him, bearing him up. Spafford catches at the rampart, drags himself up. His elbows scrape on stone as he leans into the silence, strains his eyes into the dark of the deserted garden. The palace with its empty windows, broken walls, stonework black and smashed as from a long fall, a meteorite crashed to earth.

"Horatio?" Daniel's voice is strained. "I can't—"

A queer light flickers across the garden, bright as flash-powder. The earth rocks on its axis and the palace is no longer a ruin but restored to itself, suffused with a pale fire that streams from its doors and windows to light the winter garden into flower. Spafford glimpses crocuses, irises, trees in bloom, and a fragment of birdsong drifts down from above where the great dome hovers, weightless on its columns, as he too is floating, suspended in mid-air at the moment Daniel collapses beneath him and all of the lights go out.

He strikes the pavement. The breath bursts from his lips, a standing plume, and there's a cat on the rampart above them. It bares its teeth at them, screams in its child's voice.

"A cat," Daniel says, laughing. "An accursed cat."

Spafford rolls onto his side. Across the river, the lamps of the Quai d'Orsay gleam beyond his outstretched fingers, cutting streaks down the water through which a crow passes to land on the Pont Royal. The murder has gathered there, waiting, and the Seine sweeps on beneath them through the arches of the bridge's span.

Daniel's laughing harder now, shaking with it. Shouting into the trees above them as the cat slinks away toward the palace and the murder rises in a cloud above the bridge, swarming, disappearing downriver. The laughter goes with them. The two men stand and collect themselves and Daniel offers his arm to Spafford.

"Home?" he asks.

*

Home, where Spafford dreams of black water, endless depths, a capsized vessel falling. Not the *Ville du Havre* but the Palais des Tuileries as it was before the fire with a dome for a keel and windows in rows like portholes. Anna is aboard. Her figure flickers between the lights of a long gallery, attired in white muslin, the dress she bought in Cardiff. But her hands are red, her shoulders too, and the blood rings like rain on the tiles inside as the great ship rolls and plunges, passing out of sight.

PART THREE

He wakes into another dream. Mid-afternoon on December 27th, and he is far from the boulevards, somewhere in the Twelfth Arrondissement. A hand at his coat, a child's. The fingers slim, elongated, and cropped hair coarse as straw, snarled like winterkill. It's the girl from the Place de la Madeleine, who knelt before the raving preacher in an attitude of ecstasy.

"Please," she says. "*Mon père* sent me."

He thrusts his hands into his pockets, searching for a watch that isn't there. He feels, again, the snap of the winding crown and remembers hiding the broken pieces in his nightstand. All day the hours have passed unmarked, and he is in a narrow street behind a printer's warehouse, brick walls looming up to either side.

"Your father?" he asks.

"You were there when they led him away. Don't you remember? He said I was to watch for you. To find you and bring you to him."

"What is it he wants from me?"

"You are in pain, he says. Won't you come?"

He glances left, right, up. The alley closes the sky to a strip of yellow cloud with a lone bird hovering above him. A vulture, he thinks. Waiting, watching, expectant. Same as the girl before him with her eyes wide and earnest, hopeful. *Won't you come?*

*

Mercerie, the signboard reads, but the shop is abandoned, windows punched out. The walls bulge, buckling, and the brickwork is chipped and cracking, slimed with mildew.

"Here?" Spafford asks.

"The cellar," the girl says and steals into the mouth of an adjoining alley, where a flight of stairs leads below the *mercerie*. He follows her down. The basement is surprisingly well-lit. Newspapers smolder in an iron brazier and sunlight pours from a hole in the ceiling.

Spafford asks: "This was a shop of some kind?"

"A hatmaker, yes. An old woman who never married, who had no children. She is in an asylum now, but *mon père* knew her as she was before the war."

"And she allows him to stay here?"

"No one else will come."

"Why is that?"

"They are afraid."

"Afraid?"

"The Prussian guns."

She points to the corner of the room, where shards of splintered wood mingle with twists of iron and the rim of an artillery shell is just visible, apparently intact.

"A bomb struck the shop. It smashed the roof and landed in the cellar but did not explode. The hatmaker became obsessed, insane. She could not sleep for thinking of it. But it is well, says *mon père*, there is no danger. The bomb was buried half in the earth when he found it. Like a seed he dug it up with his hands. Like a great stone he rolled it away."

Spafford, sweating, backs away toward the doorway. He steadies himself against the frame with the street behind him, the sun at his back, light without warmth.

"He is a saint, *mon père*. Like one of the prophets. Stay. You will see."

The girl sits on the floor by the brazier and crosses her legs, arranges a quilt about her shoulders. It's threadbare and torn, patched with squares of fabric she likely pilfered from the shop upstairs: umber, amber, scarlet. He sits beside her. She sprinkles shreds of newspaper over the brazier, jabs the coals with a length of twig.

The fire flickers. The dead shell glitters, black then silver.

*

Footsteps outside and the old man appears in the doorway. He's unwashed, filthy, gobbets of spit in his beard and clothes greased with horse-muck. He slips a parcel from his coat and hands it to the girl. She unfolds the brown paper to reveal a clutch of offal. Flies whirl up from the tarry lumps, forming patterns against the sunlight through which the old man passes to kneel beside the brazier.

The fire between them now. The old preacher stinks of the slaughterhouse but wears the sun's light like a halo as he addresses Spafford directly, gesticulating, speaking in Occitan. His voice is high and thin and insistent.

The girl translates. "It is good you are here. He has something he would show you."

The old man smiles. He reaches into his tattered overcoat and withdraws a small book from an inner pocket. It is the same pocket in which he carried the offal and the book's covers are smeared with brownish fingermarks. He holds it out to Spafford. "*Plaît*," he says.

"This is madness," Spafford says. "I am dreaming."

"*Plaît*," the old man says again.

Spafford takes it, opens it, nearly chokes on the odors of mold and blood that waft up from its brittle leaves. The book contains the text of the Book of Daniel in Hebrew and French with extensive footnotes, handwritten annotations citing other books and biblical passages. *Mon père*'s hand, presumably, but the script is badly cramped and nearly illegible except for columns of figures that recur throughout. Dates?

He turns to the frontispiece, an engraving that depicts a male nude with feet of clay and a golden crown. A crude pyramid has been added to the image in pencil, scratched into the man's breast in place of a heart and ringed with miniscule text that appears to show numbers, equations, measurements. Yards, feet, inches.

As a young man, Spafford attended a lecture by Charles Piazzi Smyth in which the astronomer described the use of the English inch in the pyramids' construction. This was evidence, Piazzi Smyth argued, of a direct line of descent between Melchizedek and the medieval Anglo-Saxons. *If the Great Pyramid is a text*, he said, *we are only now beginning to understand the language in which it is written. How much more has it to tell us of our creator?*

Spafford lifts the book. He squints at it through his spectacles but cannot make out the numbers on the frontispiece. Their shapes elude him, arrange themselves in spirals like a stair's down-turning, and his eyes are watering, the old man speaking more quickly than before: his lips, frothing, sweep back from his teeth to bare the rotten gums.

Again the girl translates. "He speaks of the New Jerusalem. It is here, he says, but also not here, for it is not yet as it was made. It is like this bomb. A dud, they say. A dummy. And so we may believe, but one day, yes, it will explode. This house will fall and bury us with it and what is to become of our unbelieving? That day is close, he says. Closer than we think."

"I'm sorry," Spafford says. "I don't understand."

"It is not a question of understanding. The revelation, he says, is meant for all. Many have read the prophets and pondered their meaning and always to no purpose. Prophecy is not a riddle to be unraveled but a door to be opened. It is closed, yes. Perhaps, even, it is locked. But a locked door needs only a key. He asks if you have seen the Great Pyramid?"

Spafford shakes his head.

Mon père grins. His head bobs as with tremor and he spreads his hands to form a shape like a rectangle between them. The girl nods and passes out of the light, returning with a hatbox, which she places before Spafford.

"Thank you," Spafford says, though he doesn't know why, and the old man rocks upon his heels, motions with his hands for Spafford to lift the lid, open the box.

A stereoscope.

He remembers bringing one home to the girls, years ago, how they crowded around it, taking turns: Annie first, then Maggie. She squinted into the viewfinder, closed one eye and then the other.

No, Annie said. *You're doing it wrong.*
I'm looking at the pictures.
That's what I mean. You have to look between them.
But there's nothing there.
You have to pretend. Think of anything you like.
Anything?
Picture a river.

A river, he thinks, and removes his spectacles, presses his face to the scope. Two pyramids drift into view, obscured by a sandstorm of pencil-marks. The old man babbles at him, speaking Occitan, and Spafford imagines a river between the photographs, flowing, watering the desert, until a shape emerges out of it like a flower at its opening, unfolding into three dimensions. The Great Pyramid. No longer two images but one as the pencil-marks resolve themselves into a series of measurements and formulae.

"If inches were days," the girl says. "Consider the height of the pyramid and the year that it was made. The year the Christ was born, the year he died on the cross, and the days that have passed since then. The days that are left to us before he comes again."

Spafford lifts his head. Puts on his spectacles as the girl continues to translate. "The Last Day," she says. "The Pyramid tells us of the season, even of the hour. It is close. Mon père is sure of this. The mathematics are difficult. The work is long, but the news is good. The Holy City. It is soon to be upon us, descending out of heaven."

"This world," Spafford says. His voice is ragged, hoarse, unrecognizable even to himself. "Such hell as we must endure. I cannot believe that is true."

"But *Mon père* has been there. In dreams he has seen the towers of the New Jerusalem and heard the church bells sounding. He has smelled the sweet blossoms and wandered the paths where once God walked with Adam. The gate, he says, it is not low. The way, he says, it is not narrow. All will be welcomed inside have they but eyes to see."

"No," Spafford says, and his face is in his hands, fingers to his eyes and pressing. The inner dark erupts in sparks and there's blood in his ears like ocean waves crashing.

"Not all," he says. "Not me."

A flurry of motion, then, and *Mon Père* is on his feet. His voice falls on Spafford as from a great height, shrill and stabbing.

"You are in agony," the girl translates. "In your pain you are blinded to the heart of God, which is suffering. For even death was as nothing to one who experienced incarnation, who remembered his birth. Can you imagine? His mother's body closing round him, the Living God. Her hipbones grinding, deforming his skull, pinching the cord and crushing it. The taste of his shit in his mouth. His heart slowing so he thinks that he must die and there is no release, because the pain goes on and on, unceasing, endless as his own nature and always present even after he emerges from the loving dark into a light beyond all bearing."

The voice is closer now, the old man's smell. Moldering clothes. Unwashed flesh. Sweet rot on his breath as he bends down across the stereoscope to take hold of Spafford's wrists. He pulls them apart, exposing Spafford's face and whispering into it, his closed eyes.

"The Christ was like you," the girl says. "He suffered hell that you might be spared it, and death, too, for soon there will be no more dying. The gates are open: do not remain upon the threshold. Can you hear the bells? The music? There is to be a ball tonight, as there is every night in that city where all is unending summer, never winter, and always, there is dancing."

*

Quickly, quickly, because the time is short. Afternoon deepens into twilight and the *mercerie* is behind him, the Twelfth Arrondissement. The boulevard is jammed with evening traffic, but he flags an empty cab and climbs up. "The Tuileries," he says.

The driver shakes his head. "Too late," he says. "It is closed."

Spafford digs in his pockets, produces a handful of *francs* and *centimes*.

"Well," the driver says. "Perhaps it is not so late after all."

He shouts to his team and cracks his whip, steers the carriage round a stalled omnibus. They breast a wind from the river which rips the cap from Spafford's brow, sends it spinning behind them, and the light comes red and fitful through the gaps between the buildings.

Le Tour Saint Jacques. The bell tower is all that remains of the old church. Saint-Jacques-de-la-Boucherie, it was called. Saint James of the Butchery, as on St. Bartholomew's Day, three hundred years ago, when the whole of the city reeked of blood and smoke. The breath of a thousand fires, or rather, the same great fire burning for thousands of years, consuming Eden, Chicago, the Palais des Tuileries. Ruins are knocked down, plowed into the soil. Seedlings thrust from the ground to be felled in time and fashioned into walls and bridges, palaces and cities which kindle and fall to ash, making more soil, more trees, more cities and smoke, but at last, the wheels are slowing, the cab has stopped, and they are just outside the park, its open gates.

The horses steam in the cold.

*

Dusk and the drums approaching, beating to clear the park. He crosses the horseshoe and climbs to the terrace, reaches the orangery with its Greek columns, sculpted pediment. He hides himself between the windows, presses himself to the wall so he cannot be seen from inside.

The breath streams from him as from the trees in the orangery, veiled in mist like ghosts of last summer as the drums go past and the park-sounds fade. After a time he hears the watchman's footfalls on the gravel path, followed by the rattle of a door and the man's steps in the orangery, approaching then retreating and withdrawing down the path.

Spafford follows at a distance, slips from the shadows into the city's glowering: coal-gas and firelight refract off heavy clouds, and the watchman whistles to himself, three notes, high and mournful as a mating call. The song, if it is a song, trails the watchman down the staircase to the Grand Couvert with its ranks of lime and chestnut, leafless, gray on gray and colorless but for the white marble of the Carrés d'Atalante, where the other watchmen have gathered to toss dice against the stone benches. The beams of their dark lanterns cross and double their shadows.

Night descends, the cold. Spafford kneels among the roots of a chestnut tree as the watchmen shout and laugh and stamp their feet for warmth. The church bells strike eleven, midnight. The watchmen gamble until their shift is over and it's time for them to go. Their lanterns disappear beyond the trees. The park gates open, shut, and Spafford is standing, running, his steps as swift and sure as a deer in flight.

Even the light is changing: quicksilver, sparks on magnesium. The round basin brims with it. The bronzes hold its shine, flare like beacons and light him to the private gardens of the palace, a low fence topped by steel finials. He clears it at a leap. Loses his spectacles and lands on all fours with the palace before him like a promise renewed and no evidence of the fire that destroyed it. The same storm-light fills its windows, pours into the garden and splashes among the rosebushes, sets the bare thorns blooming.

He cannot find his spectacles, doesn't need them. He passes between flowering rosebushes, crowds of ball-goers dancing together and in silence, factory workers with bankers and habited nuns with syphilitic aristocrats. Some are naked. Others wear masks. No one notices him, not even Marie Martin, dead and dripping in her gray smock with hands raised and palms flat. She dances without partner, spinning in place.

A broad staircase leads from the garden to the second floor of the palace and a row of open doors in gray-black walls. They tower over him, domed with silver like a lightning's afterimage. The ball-goers flit and spin and arrange themselves in circles around him, drawing closer, exchanging partners and moving their bodies to a music he cannot hear but must imagine, like the river that twists between two images, two cities: Paris, The New Jerusalem. *Is it well? Is it well? Is it well?*

An old Sunday School hymn. The words sung softly, only to himself, but the dancers bend their bodies to the tune and fit their steps to its rhythm, until he hears, impossibly, an echo from inside the palace, the same tune played on soft trumpets, keening strings.

"You," a woman says. "I do not know you."

Her voice is flat, faintly accented. The mumbling of a sleepwalker, Spafford thinks, but the woman is dressed for a costume ball and she's beautiful, strikingly so, green eyes in a silken mask. The Countess of Castiglione. Spafford recognizes her from the photograph in Pierre-Louis's studio.

"Countess," he says, bowing.

"Another American, then."

"Is there another?"

"Inside," she says and turns away.

He calls after her, but she doesn't turn around, drifts out of sight among the dancers. Spafford gains the terrace and approaches the staircase, begins to climb. It's only a temporary affair, evidently, fashioned from painted timbers and thronged with courtiers and servants, beggar-women in tattered petticoats and soldiers in the scarlet uniforms of the Swiss Guard. The noise is deafening. He overhears conversations in French, German, Italian, and the music is louder now, thunderous, an orchestra playing *fortissimo.*

The same song: *Is it well? Is it well? Is it well?*

Then—nothing. The voices stop, the music too, and he is inside the palace, a cavernous salon in which his steps scrape and echo. The other ball-goers are gone, all except for Anna, who sits on the floor with legs outthrust and bare feet together, four crows above her, circling.

"Anna," he says, but she doesn't hear him, doesn't see. She smiles and raises her arms before her with palms upturned, a gesture of offering. The crows descend. They rip at her hands with their beaks, parting the flesh and removing the tendons, hovering over her as they feed. Their wings beat at the air, hiding her, recalling the bloodied angel of her childhood who had found her in Gehenna, who sheltered her with wings, and she's singing as their beaks flash, black and cutting, tearing the veins from her throat and exposing the broken tube from which it comes, her voice, song. *It is well, it is well, it is well.*

*

Twisted metal, naked stone. A sky without stars. Spafford fumbles for his spectacles, but they aren't there, and the last of the revelers has long since departed. He's alone in the ruined palace, sprawled on his back in a burned-out salon. His head throbs. Pain shoots through his ankles, knees, but he takes hold of a stanchion, pulls himself up.

Four crows feed near the end of the salon. They screech as they tear at the dead thing between them, scattering feathers and clumps of fur. The body is small and shapeless, no larger than a cat. He doesn't disturb them. No moon outside and the grass is hard with frost. The cold stings his face, but he buries his chin in his collar, thrusts his hands into his coat.

Two o'clock? Three? Late, too late. His watch is broken. The planet turns and will not slow but sweeps him through the gap in the palings up Rue de Rivoli to Boulevard Malesherbes and the doors of No. 10. Inside, the apartment is quiet, dark but for a light in the guestroom. He opens the door and she's waiting for him.

"Horatio," she says.

Anna sits on the bed in her traveling clothes, a *carte-de-visite* in her hands. The portrait by Pierre-Louis. Her husband's likeness, empty as an image of his soul. "You look tired," she says, gently, and he cannot tell if she is speaking of the photograph or of himself.

"I haven't slept," he says. "Not really, not since I heard. The cable you sent."

"You work too hard."

"It was for you. Always. For them."

"I know," she says. "But there was never any need."

He turns toward her, meets her eyes, and again, he is falling, drowning. He throws himself on the bed, clings to her as to a floating spar.

She doesn't push him away. His head is in her lap. Her right arm enfolds him, resting across his collarbone and compassing his chin. Her fingertips play at his temples.

"Hush," she says. "We're here, now."

*

He opens his eyes. Minutes have passed, or hours, and neither of them has moved. Her body surrounds him: her fingers in his hair, his portrait in her hand.

"I thought you were in Versailles," he says.

"We came back tonight. The card was in the mail."

His head rolls between her thighs, cradled, and his eyes stray to the ceiling where his shadow mixes with hers, indistinguishable from it.

Anna says: "Bertha speaks very highly of Monsieur Pierson. I thought we might go tomorrow, the girls and I, when you are in Bertry."

"Bertry," he says, remembering.

Anna looks to the window where the curtains are parted, a mirrored slit of glass showing between them. "You told me once how it was for you," she begins, "when you were a boy and nearsighted. How you couldn't see the constellations. You didn't believe in them, either, not until the night you borrowed your cousin's eyeglasses. Only then were you persuaded."

"Yes."

"You understand, then, why it is we must go."

He lifts his head out of her lap. "Go?"

"To Pierson's," she says. "For even now you do not see them. And because you do not see them, you cannot believe in them. And because you do not believe in them, you cannot hear them, their voices, though they sing to you in the night."

"Anna, don't."

"I remember reading once of Mrs. Lincoln's visit to Mr. Mumler, the photographer. She gave him a false name, of course, but he developed the plate, and her husband was plainly visible. He stood with his hands at her shoulders to give comfort. The camera saw what she herself could not, and she understood that she was not, in fact, bereaved. That God would not be so cruel as to part her from her beloved. That she had not, in fact, lost anything at all."

The bedroom judders and spins, the girls or their shadows like birds' wings beating close. He feels himself sinking. Slides to the floor with a weight on his chest and Anna's voice above him. "Your coat," she says. "You had a picture inside. A woman. Her eyes were closed, and I couldn't imagine who she was or why you had it, not until tonight when the package came from Pierson. I thought of the two photographs, of Mumler's images, and I realized at last how you, too, might be saved."

"Saved," he says. The word like sawdust in his mouth as he steadies himself against the dresser, wincing as the wound in his palm splits open. He stands and steps between the window and the light, eclipsing their reflections. "They weren't saved, Anna. They're gone."

Her expressions remains tranquil, becalmed with a child's confidence of love, Tanetta's eyes in hers meeting his as she shakes her head and addresses him with a tenderness he has not heard in years. "You haven't changed," she says. "Forty-five years old and you are still that poor, nearsighted boy, who would not believe in anything he couldn't see. You speak so eloquently of faith, having none yourself, and you will not trust me as I once trusted you. That place, Wanamingo, the year I spent there. Do you remember? I returned to Chicago but could not leave it behind me. Could not believe in a God of Love or imagine a future for myself. Not until that morning in Sunday School when I heard you speak of grace and the surety of salvation. I trusted you, Horatio, and for a time, that was enough. You asked for my hand, and I did not refuse you, but you were never mine, not in truth. These last two years you have wanted only to be free of me. I was to you a burden, a mouth to be fed and kept quiet. A body to be clothed and sometimes touched when your own need became too great."

"You abandoned me."

"No."

"You can't imagine what it was like. How I suffered."

"Tanetta's birth. The great fire. Every night afterward I found myself back in Gehenna, in winter, when the air tastes sharp as gall. It stops your breath. Gets into your bones, they say, and maybe they're right. Because I lingered over the stove and could never get warm."

"I tried to help you," Spafford says. "This trip, our passage on the *Ville du Havre*. You don't know what it cost me, the price I paid…"

"You did not go with us."

"It couldn't be helped."

"Business, you said."

"We would have lost everything."

"We did," she says, smiling, and he cannot understand her.

He turns away. He wipes at his brow with his injured hand, smearing warm blood into his lashes so the bedroom swims with it, his face in the window red-sheened like a murderer's with nail-holes for eyes and the mouth hanging open, another wound.

*

I remember only fragments, Anna says. The girls clinging to my nightgown. The roar of the sea as it rushed at us. Annie's voice in my ear, whispering. *Don't be afraid*, she said. *The sea is His and He made it.* The waves washing over me, their awful cold. Tanetta crushed to my chest as I kicked against the tide, its pull on us, until a spar cracked my elbow and I let go. I woke up alone, floating face down on the same spar. My right arm trailed in the water, bruised and numb, holding nothing where once it held my heart. Splinters dug into my face, and the night above me swarmed with points of light, stars in strange constellations and meteors trailing fire, a line of four stars falling.

Above me, I thought, but I was wrong. I couldn't see the sky, only its reflection on the water. The stars weren't above me but someplace far below, fathoms deep, blazing like suns as they rose out of the depths. They streaked toward me, broke the surface with a flurry of wings. The water roiled and dashed me in spray, but I wasn't cold. The girls warmed me with their new bodies, their feathers on my flesh and Tanetta's beak at my breast, suckling.

The sea is His, Annie said, and it is. He giveth and He taketh away and the ocean that devoured our children clothed them in feathers and starlight. The spar, too. It smashed my arm and stole my baby, and it saved me from dying because I couldn't let it go. Madness, you might call that, but your hands are empty, Horatio, and the night is passing. The children do not belong to us but to their Father in Heaven. They must fly to him, and soon, and you will be left adrift and drowning, never knowing it was all around you, such a light.

*

Rainfall, early dawn. A black sky deepening to violet, cut with darker veins that twist like rivers, open to a place he cannot reach. His train is due, but Spafford lingers on the steps outside No. 10, looking up. His vision blurs, straining, and he imagines a glimpse of silver gates above him, closed, a palace caged in bars of rain.

Six o'clock. Church bells strike to sound the hour, but there are no trumpets to give answer. Only the sound of rain and the voice he heard in his dreaming, Anna cooing to her birds as they tore her apart. *It is well, it is well, it is well.*

The image flickers and dissolves, shivered to pieces by the roar that follows.

An exploding shell, he thinks, but no, it's only thunder.

PART FOUR

He arrives in Bertry, makes his way to the Poulain house. Théo is staying there. The young pastor's in-laws live outside the village in a stone-built farmhouse with an adjoining chapel hewn from timber. The family's wealth is considerable. Héliodore Poulain, Théo's father-in-law, owns a mill in Bertry where wool is carded and spun and woven into textiles to be shipped to Paris and sold at the family's storefront in Rue Aboukir.

Théo is away, it seems, called out unexpectedly, but his wife Simée invites Spafford inside and shows him around the house. Parlor, study, gunroom. The kitchen where a black-clad Héliodore Poulain butchers a lamb in his Sunday best while Théo's son Georges rocks in the cradle behind him and Georges's older sister Ellen sits cross-legged on the rug, playing with a blue-eyed doll, talking to herself as she brushes down its hair.

Simée leads Spafford into a paneled vestibule at the rear of the house with a door that opens into a walled garden, grass-tips gleaming, then past a coat tree hung with oilskins and across the Poulain family chapel to a narrow staircase. He follows her upstairs to a low-ceilinged attic with two small rooms in which the Lorriaux children sleep and a third bedroom at the end of the corridor. "Madame Spafford stayed there," Simée says. "When first she came."

"Show me," he says.

The room is small and square and windowless, comprising a bedframe and washbasin, little more, and the walls are unfinished, un-plastered. He hears the rain through them, hears wind in the rafters.

"She was so cold," Simée says. "I helped her to bed and went to fetch another blanket. When I came back, she was asleep and would not stir. I looked in often, but she appeared at peace, and Théo said we mustn't wake her. After twenty hours, she awoke, and she was different somehow, changed. The things she said, the songs she sang. *Is well, is well.* You know it, perhaps, monsieur?"

He shakes his head, doesn't speak.

*

Twilight, falling, steals the color from the day, and Théo returns to the Poulain house. He apologizes for his absence and ushers Spafford into the chapel, the long table where dinner is served. The other men already are seated, all except Héliodore, but they offer him no acknowledgment, saying nothing to Spafford or even to each other as Simée readies the table with wineglasses and silver and the boy Georges riding at her hip.

The rain has stopped and all sound with it but for clinking crystal, baby's breath, a flurry of rapid footsteps as the girl Ellen pelts into the room with her doll dragging behind her. "It's snowing," she says, and asks to go out, but Simée won't allow it. "Look after Georges," Simée says and sets the baby down beside his sister.

Simée pours wine. A candle winks out overhead, dimming the room, and she mounts the table with a rushlight, stretches to reach the chandelier. The small flame wavers, and the trembling spreads to her arms, knees. Théo stands and places his hand against her back, steadying her. She smiles and opens her mouth, as if to thank him, but she doesn't, dismounts the table without speaking as Héliodore enters the chapel, bringing in the lamb. He carries the roast to his place at the head of the table and raises the steam-wreathed salver as in offering. He intones a blessing, presents the slaughtered lamb.

"Amen," they all say.

Silence, again, but Ellen is three years old, no longer content to go unnoticed. She lifts her infant brother by his armpits and carries him about the room giggling. Georges makes no protest. He trusts his sister completely, it seems, though with scant enough cause, and he's laughing even as the girl stumbles, falls, and lets him go.

*

Snow. A dusting, only that, but more is falling, wide flakes turning over and over in the light from the windows as they trudge across the walled garden, Théo first, then Spafford behind him. Their footsteps crack like glass, and Spafford hears bleating ewes, a wagon passing on the highway. Children's voices. Ellen? Georges?

Théo pauses at the gate. It's black and intricate, wrought iron like the fences round the Tuileries and opening onto a field or pasture, wide and white and climbing to a wooded ridge. "There's a shepherd's path," Théo says. "The distance is not great. Two miles, perhaps, if we follow it to the end. The road will take us back."

"Lead on," Spafford says, and Théo lets them out.

The garden is behind them, the chapel too. Spafford cannot discern the path, but Théo proceeds with confidence along the pasture's margin. They crest the ridgeline, continue along it, and the shepherd's flock is visible below, their humped outlines, black on black in this light like the road to Bertry and the canal that runs alongside.

"Simée brought me upstairs," Spafford says. "She showed me Anna's room."

"She stayed with us a few days only. Most of that time she slept."

"Twenty hours, Simée said."

"More than that. She was exhausted."

"Simée said she was different when she awoke. That she had changed."

Théo exhales. "We put in at Cardiff," he says, "after the wreck. We sent our cables and afterward the company purchased for us mourning attire. Anna would not wear black but took down instead from a higher shelf a bolt of white muslin. At the time, I thought it strange, but now, I wonder if that isn't when it started, when she first heard them."

"Her birds," Spafford says.

"She did not speak of them," Théo says. "Not then. Not until the morning she awoke and we heard her laughter from the attic room. She was speaking with them, your girls. Singing with them too. The same song, always, though we did not know it. The days passed and she was worse. More and more she talked to them, only them, and sometimes, at night, she kept the house awake with her singing. Around this time, she received a letter from Paris."

"Bertha Johnston."

"She showed me the letter. She asked me what I thought."

"What did you say?"

"That she must do as she wished. That she should go."

Théo slows his pace as they approach a copse of evergreens, fir trees mingled with spruce and a flat rock thrusting from the snow-cover. Théo sits down on it, settles his weight. Spafford joins him. Their breath drifts into the branches.

"I am sorry, Horatio," Théo says. "I did not know what else to do. She was sickening, retreating inward, losing weight. The children were afraid of her."

Motion overhead: a shadow, an owl. It swoops from the copse to light on a stone in the field below.

"You needn't apologize," Spafford says. "You did nothing wrong."

"I should have helped her."

"You did."

"Or tried harder to understand."

"It would have made no difference."

"No? How can you be certain?"

"She told me everything."

"Everything?"

"And still I know nothing."

He tells Théo of the shipwreck, what Anna said, the stars that rose out of the depths. Théo listens, watchful, then rises to his feet, blows into his cupped hands. The steam runs between his fingers, trailing away, and he turns back toward Spafford.

"No, Horatio," he says. "That is not how it was."

*

Twelve minutes, Théo says. That is all. We were struck at two o'clock. Twelve minutes later, we were in the water. The English sailors took me aboard their ship and I watched from the railing as the lifeboats went out, came back. After half-an-hour, a man shouted up from below. *We have a woman*, he said, speaking English, and directed his lantern's beam to the stern of the boat, where Anna slumped between two oarsmen. Her nightgown was in tatters and there was blood in her hair. They could not rouse her, but one of the men took her over his shoulder with her arms hanging down and climbed the ropes carrying her.

Her eyes were closed. She was very still. The second mate asked if I knew her, and I said that I did. We carried her below-decks to the mate's cabin, wide enough only for the cot on which we laid her. Her clothes are wet, the mate said. She will freeze. He opened his trunk and removed a nightshirt and a pair of trousers and turned his back as I changed her clothes and covered her with a blanket. Eventually, he returned to his post while I stayed with her until her breathing slowed and steadied.

I went back on deck. The boats had returned, and the Captain would send no more. His own ship was in danger of sinking, he said, and all hands were needed if they were to prevent a second disaster. I followed him to the deck-rail, where he watched the final boat being unloaded. I pleaded with him to go out again. The children, I said. The little ones. But the Captain shook his head. Too cold, he said. Too late.

Anna heard what he said, understood what it meant. She had made her way on deck and was behind us all the time though we did not know of it, not until she struck the rail between us with her body and would have gone over if the mate's shirt had not caught on a jutting bolt. The fabric stretched and tore and the Captain grabbed at her long hair, pulling her back. She tried again to jump, but my arms were around her now, pressing her arms to her sides as I tried to keep her still.

Useless, of course. She screamed and wept and would not be comforted. Shh, I said, but she would not quieten. They are with Him, I said, the God who made them, and she cried because it was not true, she would not believe it.

*

The owl flies off. The snow is lighter now and Bertry is visible from the copse. Troisville, too, and Clary. A line of villages like shore-lights blazing and the snow-black land between them flowing, turning, rushing toward the ridge as the wind shifts direction and the countryside dissolves in a haze of blowing ice. Théo and Spafford retreat into the fir trees, rustling branches like murmuring waves, the sea at night, 47°21'N 35°31'W.

"This field," Théo says. "My wife's family acquired it some years ago, but they allow the previous owner to graze his flock here. He takes his luncheon in this grove. On this rock, usually. He told me about it once. An altar, he called it. The Gauls had sacrificed their children here, he said, and showed me the channels down which it had poured, the blood of innocents."

Théo clears snow from the rock, revealing a map of shallow grooves carved into its surface. "Simée laughed when I told her. This stone, she assures me, is nothing more sinister than an old grindstone recovered from a mill that once stood here. Shepherds are a practical people, she said, having time only for the present moment, the flocks they watch and are always counting. What use to them is history? The past? It is a dream, she said, a story to be told and retold and changed at every telling. And later that night, lying awake, I thought on the eve of His Nativity and of the shepherds that bore Him witness. I wondered if they had ever learned of His death on the cross. If they recalled that night in the stable three decades before and remembered an angel when there was none, not then, but after?"

Spafford looks away, looks down. His hands, upturned. The bandage he wears and the gash beneath it, black through white like channels in the shepherd's table. He touches his fingers to the chiseled stone. Thinks of Anna, the stories she tells, told. Birds of fire, stars from the sea. A feral woman garbed in rags and wings. They are fragments of dreaming like photographs of the dead or *mon père*'s New Jerusalem. His own vision of the Tuileries restored: a song in the night where there was only silence, winter. The weight of water. An old man's brass teeth.

*

They walk a little farther, return by the Troisvilles road. A quarter mile from Bertry and they hear bells, smell smoke. Théo quickens his pace, Spafford too, and they round a bend to find the Poulain House in flames, the chapel engulfed, its windows cracking then shattering as the house-bell clangs and clangs. The fire-wagon hasn't yet arrived from Bertry, but a line of volunteers reaches from the doorway to the canal across the road where men fill buckets and hand them along, their every movement dwarfed by their shadows on the stone façade.

The snow melts and falls as rain, steams into nothingness. Théo approaches the bucket-line at run. One of the men waves him toward the house and he takes off sprinting for the garden at the rear of the house. Spafford follows him, finds Théo wrestling with Simée. She claws at her husband, wailing, as the fire hisses and booms, an inrushing tide.

The attic, he thinks. Ellen. Georges. He runs to the back door and is halfway through when the heat slams against him, driving him back. He strips off his coat. Draws it over his head to rush the door a second time and crash into the vestibule. The house shakes. The ceiling rains down sparks that settle on his overcoat, igniting the fabric. He tears it off, blistering his hands and unhooking an oilskin from the coat tree. He covers his head with it, continues into the chapel, where all is inferno, timber and beam alight and flames in black waves, rolling, flowing up the walls and across the ceiling. He swims through the fire like a man dreaming and is at the staircase, climbing, when a portion of the roof collapses and he is blown back into the chapel.

He strikes the table, sprawls on the floor. His hands crack and bubble and there's smoke in his eyes as he catches at a table-leg, pulls himself upright. The oilskin melts into his hair and he lets it fall away. He stumbles forward, making for the stair though he cannot breathe, cannot see, hears nothing but the roar of the fire and a faint voice from behind him, louder now, someone shouting his name. Théo. He takes Spafford by the arm, wrestles him outside into the garden. "The children," Spafford says.

"Shh."

"I couldn't reach them."

"They are safe, Horatio."

"But—Simée—"

"She put them to bed after supper. She thought they were upstairs, but Ellen had sneaked outside with Georges. She wanted him to see the snow."

"Where—?"

"They were in the garden. Ellen heard her mother screaming and thought she would be punished. She hid with Georges beyond the gate. They were not in the house."

Spafford laughs, coughs. He hears the fire-wagon coming closer, bringing pump and hose. Théo says he must speak with them, asks if Spafford is injured?

He shakes his head, watches Théo go. Unhurt, he thinks. Another lie. His hands are blackened, bloodied, the old wound seeping through its bandage. The lungs burn in his chest, but the garden gate is open, swinging on its hinges with Simée beyond it, pacing, making circles in the snow with the baby Georges in her arms, passing his weight from left hip to right, while Ellen follows, dancing, leaping between her mother's footprints, going nowhere.

Around and around, but the planet's hold is failing. Spafford rises, drifts out of the garden and across the road, passing bucket-line and fire-wagon, horses and pump. He stands over the canal with the water below him, black and frothing. The fire pump draws against the current, reversing its flow, and there are sparks in the air like snowflakes pouring upward, slowing their ascent to hang above him in constellations. The Pleiades. Orion, the hunter. The river Eridanus into which he falls with arms outstretched and reaching for the water, its stillness, so close.

ACKNOWLEDGMENTS

"A Song in the Night" is indebted, principally, to the American Colony in Jerusalem Collection at the Library of Congress, accessible online at https://www.loc.gov/collections/american-colony-in-jerusalem. Additional information concerning the lives of the Spaffords, the events of 1871, and the 1873 wreck of the *Ville du Havre* is derived from various primary and secondary sources, including:

Corts, Thomas E. *Seeking Solace: The Life and Legacy of Horatio G. Spafford*. Samford University Press, 2014.

Geniesse, Jane Fletcher. *American Priestess: The Extraordinary Story of Anna Spafford and the American Colony in Jerusalem*. Nan A. Talese, 2008.

Hill, Michael. *Elihu Washburne: The Diary and Letters of America's Minister to France During the Siege and Commune of Paris*. Simon & Schuster, 2012.

Vester, Bertha Spafford. *Our Jerusalem: An American Family in the Holy City, 1881-1949*. Doubleday & Company, 1950.

Weiss, Nathanaël. *Personal Recollections of the Wreck of the Ville du Havre and the Loch-Earn*. Anson D. F. Randolph & co., 1875.

A Song in the Night
by Daniel Mills

First ZAGAVA paperback edition
edited and published by
Jonas J. Ploeger

ZAGAVA®
in the summer of 2024

Text: © Daniel Mills
Artwork: © Julia Nau
Frontispiece photo courtesy of
The United States Library of Congress

Text set in Minion Pro
Titles set in Roadway
Design and typeset by Jan-Marco Schmitz

All rights reserved.

www.zagava.de

ISBN 978-3-949341-70-0

A SONG IN THE NIGHT

was published as *limited numbered* & *limited lettered* hardcover as well.

WWW.ZAGAVA.DE

Manufactured by Amazon.ca
Bolton, ON

40063247R00049